The Great Barrier Reef

Debbie Croft
Illustrations by Nathalie Ortega

Contents

The Reef

The Great Barrier Reef is the largest coral reef system in the world. It is located in the Coral Sea, off the coast of Australia. It begins at the tip of Cape York in the north, and stretches 3000 kilometres south along the Queensland coast. The reef lies between 15 and 150 kilometres offshore. In some places, it is 65 kilometres wide.

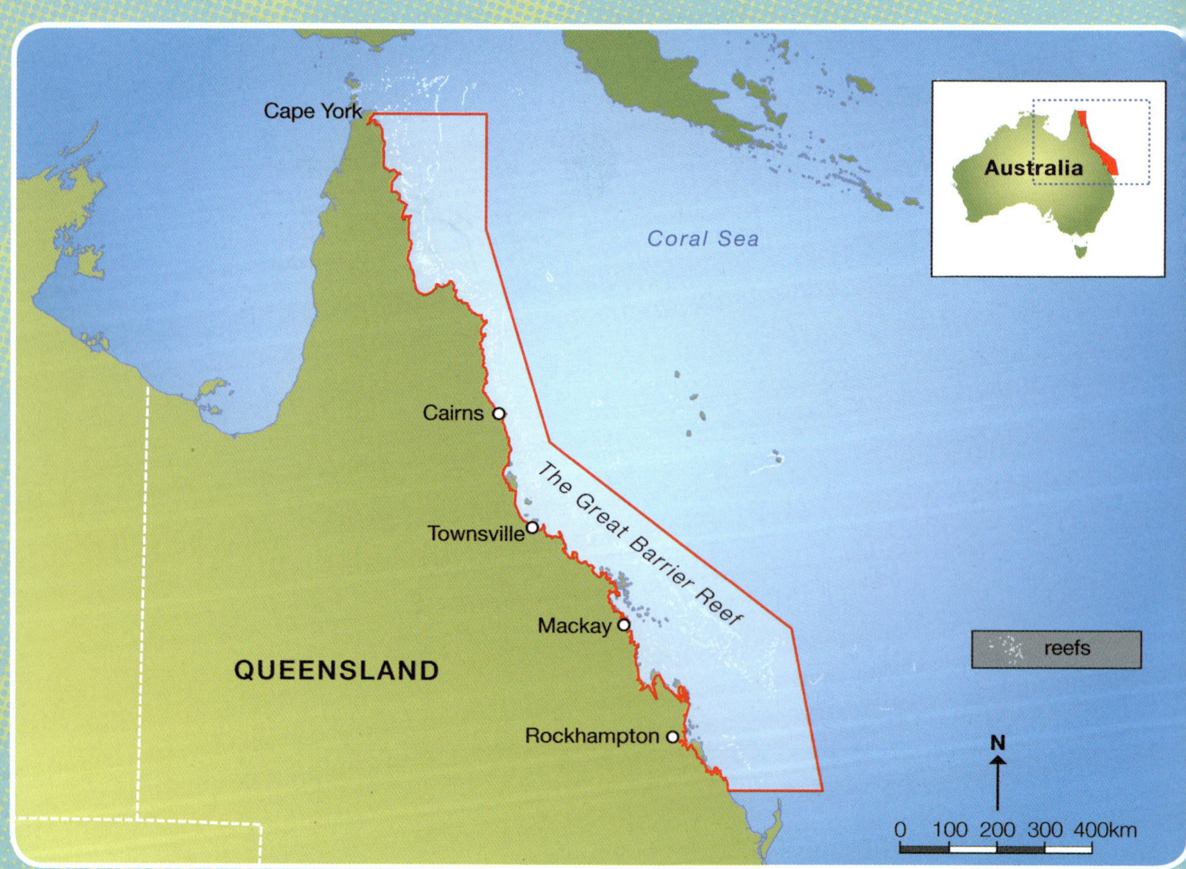

Think and Talk About ...
The Great Barrier Reef is the only living thing on Earth that can be seen from space.

This reef is the world's largest single structure made by living creatures. There are almost 600 different types of coral on the Great Barrier Reef. Together, they create an impressive display of colour that has made this environment well known throughout the world.

Coral reefs need sunlight to grow, so they are mainly found in clear waters up to 60 metres deep. Because some types of coral look like trees, reefs are sometimes called "rainforests of the sea".

Brain coral got its name because it resembles the human brain.

Types of Coral

The two main types of coral on the Great Barrier Reef are hard coral and soft coral.

Hard coral forms when groups of **polyps** make **limestone** skeletons to support themselves. Usually, a single hard coral is made up of hundreds, thousands or millions of coral polyps. These polyps live together as a **colony**. The two most common types of hard coral in the Great Barrier Reef are “brain coral” and “staghorn coral”.

Staghorn coral grows extremely quickly.

Soft coral does not have a skeleton. Its body is soft and jelly-like, so it looks more like a plant. Tiny limestone spikes provide support and protection for soft coral.

Soft coral is often bright pink and mauve, but these vivid colours are not usually seen in hard coral.

A variety of fish, prawns and sea slugs live in the branches of soft coral. The coral provides excellent **camouflage** because it has the same colours and patterns as these creatures. Some soft coral is in danger of being eaten by marine animals.

The Hinge-beak Shrimp (above) and the Longnose Hawkfish (below) are camouflaged by the coral in the Great Barrier Reef.

Think and Talk About ...
Some types of coral make a poison that has an unpleasant taste for predators.

Clownfish are named for their bright colours.

Marine Life

A variety of marine life lives in the Great Barrier Reef. There are hundreds of different species of fish, sea snakes, sea turtles and sea grasses. Some creatures, including the dugong and the Green Sea Turtle, are **endangered**. Saltwater crocodiles live in the mangrove swamps along the coast near the reef. Humpback Whales also use the reef as a breeding area when they migrate from the Antarctic.

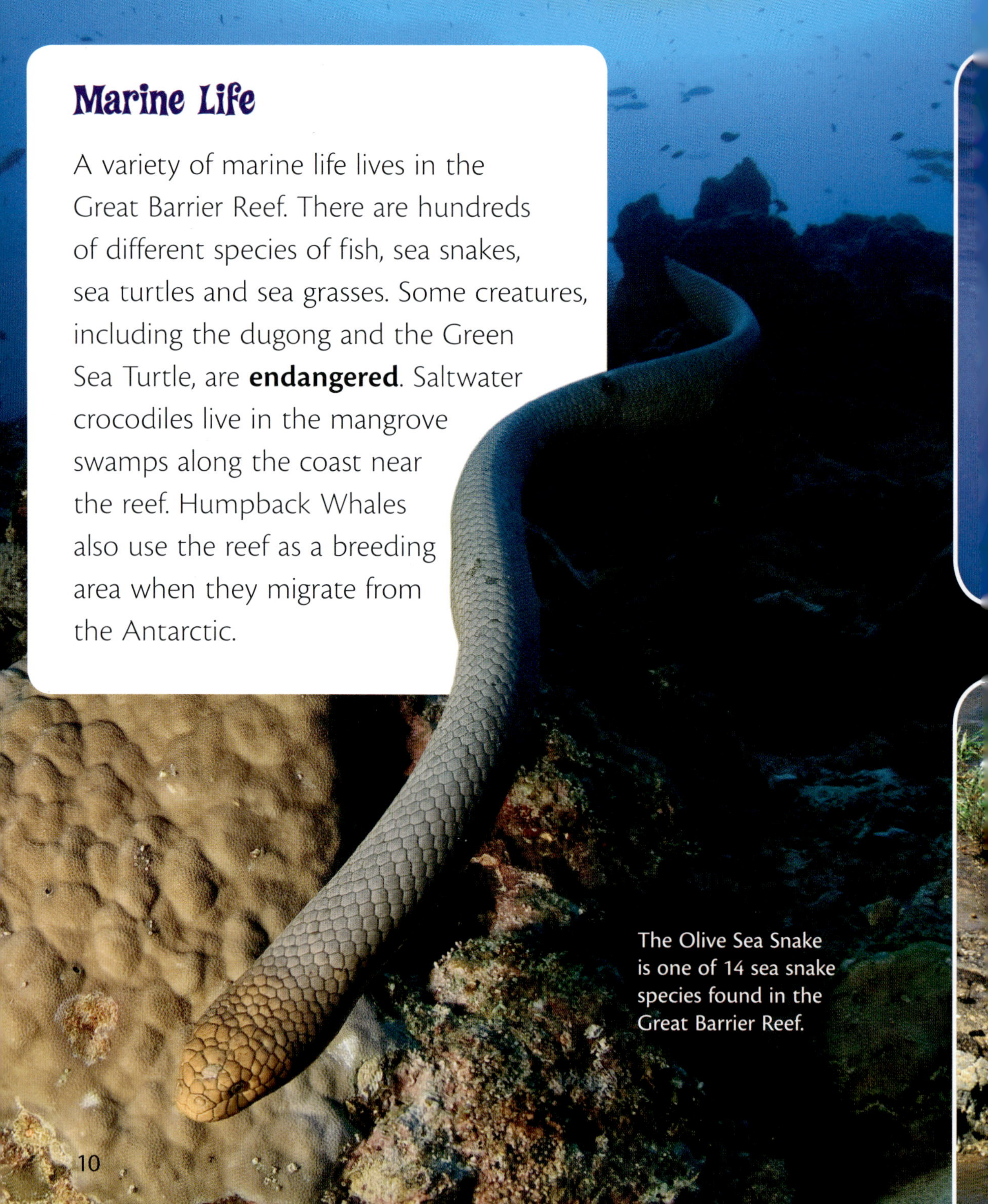

The Olive Sea Snake is one of 14 sea snake species found in the Great Barrier Reef.

The Humpback Whale migrates to the Great Barrier Reef from Antarctic waters.

The saltwater crocodile lives along the coast.

Aboriginal and Torres Strait Islander Peoples

Aboriginal and Torres Strait Islander peoples have known about, and used, the Great Barrier Reef for more than 60 000 years. They developed a great knowledge of the environment in this area.

Before Europeans came to Australia, Aboriginal and Torres Strait Islander peoples journeyed through the reef to trade with other Indigenous groups along the coast. They travelled in canoes and used the wind and the stars to find their way.

Aboriginal and Torres Strait Islander peoples have been fishing in the Great Barrier Reef for thousands of years.

Think and Talk About ...

Many traditional dances and songs convey stories about the reefs and islands.

A World Heritage Site

The Great Barrier Reef was made a World Heritage Site in 1981. This means the reef must be protected for people to enjoy in the future. A large part of the reef is also protected by the Great Barrier Reef Marine Park Authority, which helps to reduce the effects of activities such as fishing and tourism.

An employee of the Great Barrier Reef Marine Park Authority holds a rescued turtle.

Think and Talk About ...

The Great Barrier Reef is one of the Seven Natural Wonders of the World.

Risks to the Reef

There are many things that put the survival of the Great Barrier Reef at risk. Some of these include tropical cyclones, the Crown-of-Thorns Starfish, pollution, fishing, oil spills and changes to the climate.

Tropical Cyclones

When tropical cyclones occur along the coast, they can cause serious damage to the reef. Strong winds disturb the shallow water and can snap pieces of coral off the reef. Then these pieces get tossed around the ocean floor and thrown into deeper water.

Cyclone damage has destroyed a lot of coral in the Great Barrier Reef.

Crown-of-Thorns Starfish

The Crown-of-Thorns Starfish preys on coral polyps. Sometimes, the number of starfish increases naturally. At other times, too many of its predators are caught, and more starfish survive. If this happens in one particular area, large sections of the reef can be damaged or destroyed.

Think and Talk About ...

A female Crown-of-Thorns Starfish can produce up to 65 million eggs in a season.

The Crown-of-Thorns Starfish preys mostly on hard coral.

Pollution

Land near the Great Barrier Reef is used for growing sugar cane and grazing cattle. Most pollution in the reef is caused by **runoff** from these farms. When it rains, chemicals wash into the waters near the reef, damaging the plants and animals.

The Great Barrier Reef is polluted by runoff from farms when it rains.

Think and Talk About ...

Every year, huge numbers of seabirds die as a result of plastics being discarded in their environment.

Fishing

Fishing is a favourite activity for many visitors to the reef. However, huge **trawlers** can damage areas of the reef by dragging nets through the water to catch prawns and fish to sell.

A fishing trawler searches for prawns in the Great Barrier Reef.

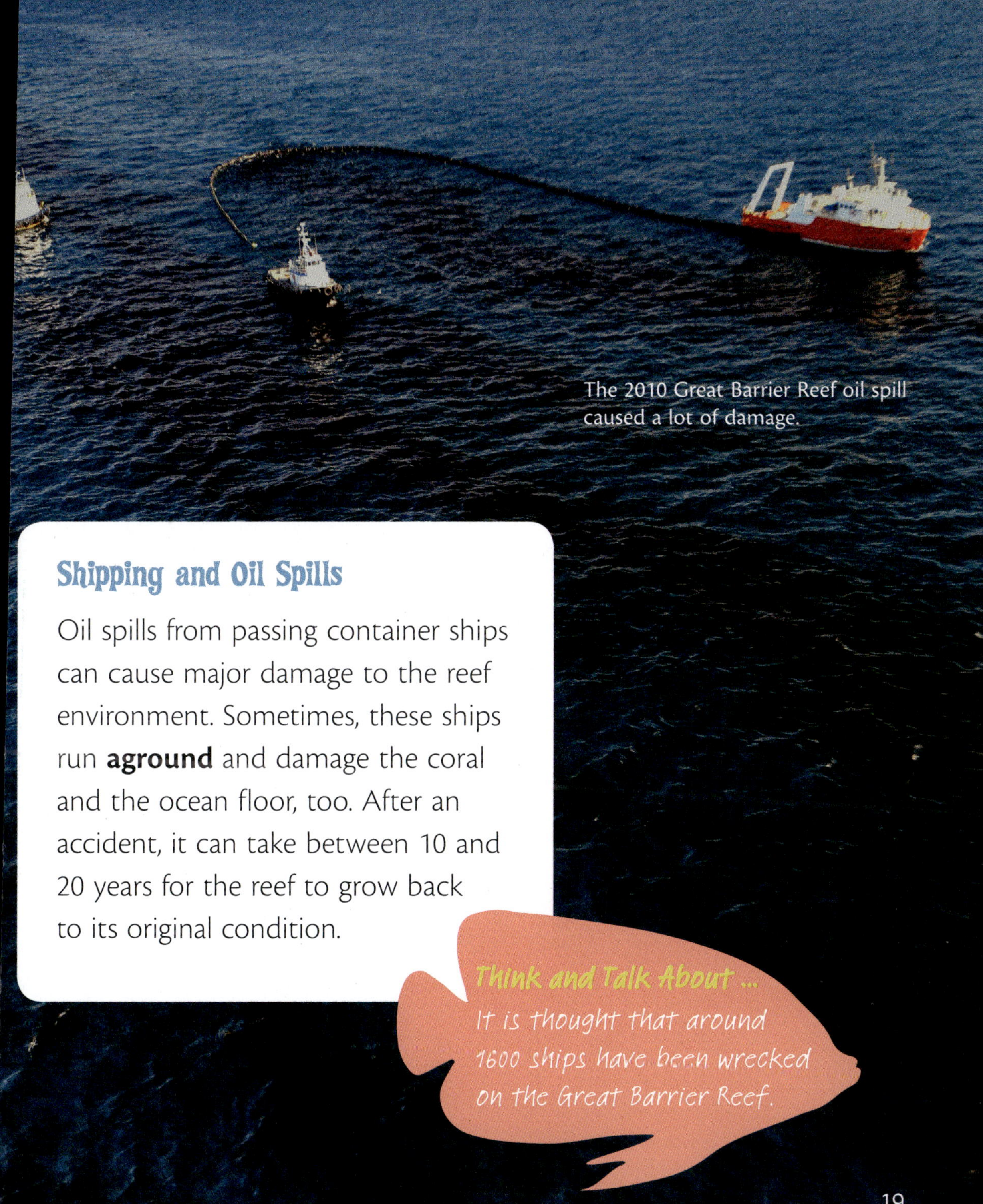

The 2010 Great Barrier Reef oil spill caused a lot of damage.

Shipping and Oil Spills

Oil spills from passing container ships can cause major damage to the reef environment. Sometimes, these ships run **aground** and damage the coral and the ocean floor, too. After an accident, it can take between 10 and 20 years for the reef to grow back to its original condition.

Think and Talk About ...

It is thought that around 1600 ships have been wrecked on the Great Barrier Reef.

Climate Change

Scientists at the Marine Park Authority believe the greatest risk to the reef is **climate change**. An increase in the water temperature can cause coral to lose its colour. **Algae** live inside the **tissue** of coral, and provide energy for it to grow. They also give coral its colour. However, these algae cannot survive in warmer water and, without them, the coral appears white.

This coral's loss of colour is caused by an increase in water temperature.

The Great Barrier Reef is a very important habitat for many species of plants and animals. It is also a famous tourist attraction for visitors from all around the world. However, without careful planning and protection, the Great Barrier Reef's natural beauty can easily be destroyed.

Snorkelling on the Reef

As we walked onto the jetty from the small island where we had stayed overnight, I sensed this outing was going to be something very special. Our guide helped everyone board a sightseeing boat that took us along a section of the reef.

The boat was simple in its design. Passengers sat along each side, in a single row, facing the centre. Dad and I sat on one side of the boat, and Mum and my older sister, Isla, sat opposite us. The bottom of the boat was made from a type of clear, hardened plastic. In this part of our tour, we would be able to see the underwater world of the Great Barrier Reef without getting wet!

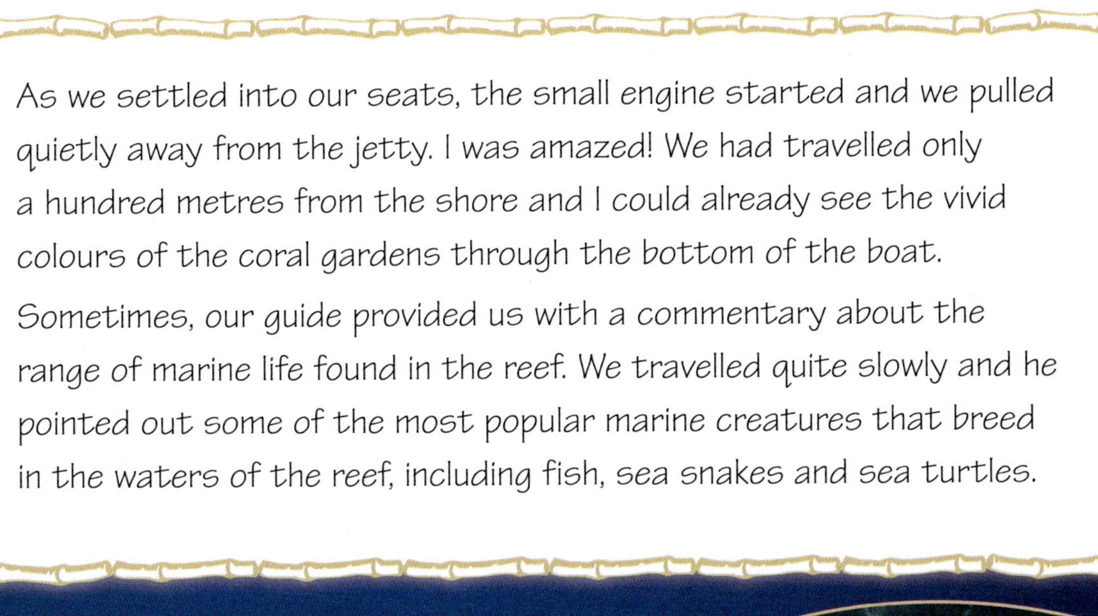

As we settled into our seats, the small engine started and we pulled quietly away from the jetty. I was amazed! We had travelled only a hundred metres from the shore and I could already see the vivid colours of the coral gardens through the bottom of the boat.

Sometimes, our guide provided us with a commentary about the range of marine life found in the reef. We travelled quite slowly and he pointed out some of the most popular marine creatures that breed in the waters of the reef, including fish, sea snakes and sea turtles.

I was delighted when our guide pointed out the clownfish in the shallow water. They were a bright orange colour, with white bars on their bodies. They were quite small, only about ten centimetres long. We watched them dart in and out among the waving tentacles of the anemones where they lived.

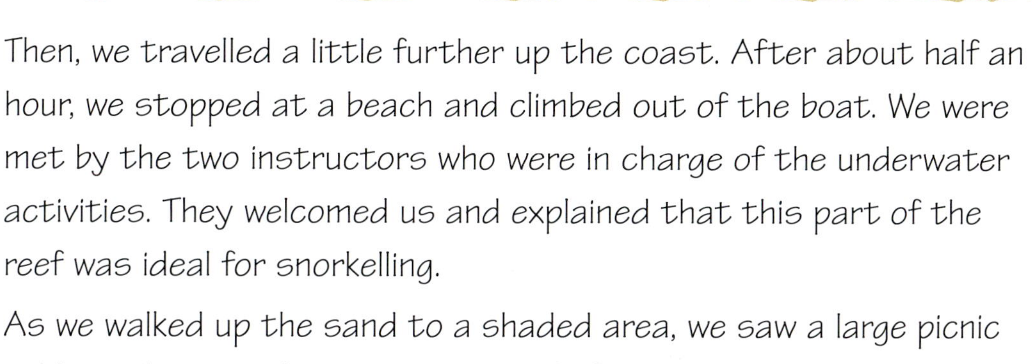

Then, we travelled a little further up the coast. After about half an hour, we stopped at a beach and climbed out of the boat. We were met by the two instructors who were in charge of the underwater activities. They welcomed us and explained that this part of the reef was ideal for snorkelling.

As we walked up the sand to a shaded area, we saw a large picnic table, with a mouth-watering spread of delicious food. There were fresh sandwiches and a selection of juicy, tropical fruits, which we were invited to share.

After lunch, we spent some time learning about snorkelling. Isla and I had never taken part in this type of activity before. We were really excited at the idea of swimming through the shallow waters to see the coral and marine life. It was an excellent place to experience the wonders of the reef because it allowed us to “surface snorkel”. This meant we needed to use only basic equipment.

We listened carefully while the instructors explained how to use the flippers, mask and snorkel. Then they reminded us about basic safety when swimming in the open water. They also talked about why we should protect the reef by not touching the coral. When this part of our training was complete, they described some of the magnificent underwater scenes we would see. I wanted to start straight away, but Mum insisted we practise breathing through our snorkels first!

Then we put on our wetsuits so we didn't get stung by jellyfish. We waded out a short distance. I was in water that was only waist deep. It was fascinating! Just by bending over and putting my mask on the surface of the water, I had an incredible view of this marine environment. The pink and purple colours of the coral were quite striking! Isla saw a school of clownfish and motioned for me to look at them. There were about seven of them swimming along together, all with the same stunning orange-and-white markings.

Before long, Isla wanted to swim out a little further, so Mum and Dad encouraged me to go, too. Most of the time we just floated on our stomachs, kicking our legs to move us slowly along. We had been told to tread water when we needed a rest, so we didn't accidentally stand on the coral. In this area, we saw some larger species of fish, and some different varieties of coral. It really was a spectacular sight! We swam around for over an hour, before heading back into the shore. The instructors collected our masks, flippers and snorkels and we boarded the small boat once more.

We all agreed that this had been an amazing experience and that it was a perfect way to enjoy the beauty and mystery of the Great Barrier Reef!

Glossary

aground (*adverb*)	a boat that has run aground has become stuck in shallow water
algae (*noun*)	very small plants that grow in the water
camouflage (*noun*)	a way of hiding by looking the same as the surroundings
climate change (*noun*)	a big change in climate conditions, such as Earth getting warmer
colony (*noun*)	a group of animals or plants that live together
endangered (*adjective*)	in danger of dying out
limestone (*noun*)	a hard, white rock
polyps (*noun*)	small sea animals that have tube-shaped bodies
runoff (*noun*)	excess water that flows from places such as farms
tissue (*noun*)	a group of cells that a living thing is made of
trawlers (*noun*)	very large boats used for fishing

Index